Looking For Holes

For Campbell,
and thanks to Meryn, Brad,
and especially my mother — N.S.

For Gill and Sarah — G.C.

First published by Douglas & McIntyre, Toronto
First United States Edition

10 9 8 7 6 5 4 3 2 1

CIP data available upon request.
ISBN 1-879085-92-5

Whispering Coyote Press, Inc.
480 Newbury Street
Suite 104
Danvers, MA 01923

Designed by Michael Solomon
Set in Adobe Stone Serif and Monotype Grotesque
by Pixel Graphics, Toronto
Illustrated in Gouache and watercolor
on watercolor paper
Printed and bound in Hong Kong
by Everbest Printing Co. Ltd.

Alexander Salamander

Alexander Salamander
Lives beneath a stone.
He comes out every Tuesday
'Cause he hasn't got a phone.

We meet down by the river
On the beaver's pile of sticks
Where he shows me tads of tadpoles
And insect-catching tricks.

He feeds me breaded dragonflies
And hot mosquito crunch …
I think, perhaps, that next week
I'll visit *after* lunch!

Derek the Dragon

Derek the Dragon is draggin' his feet,
His mood is so tragically bleak
That he cries steamy teardrops that boil and bubble
And burn when they touch his cheek.

Every time that he giggles or gurgles or grumbles
Or mutters or sputters or shouts,
Every time that he yawns or he opens his mouth
A fiery flame rushes out.

He's eaten an iceberg, he's sipped up the sea,
He lived in my freezer for days.
He eats fire engines, he swallows them whole
But his barbecue breath still stays.

So Derek the Dragon is draggin' his feet,
He's as low as an empty tire.
'Cause it's hard to be happy if you are a dragon
And not very fond of fire.

Wednesday Morning Worms

If your fingers have the fiddles
And your legs have got the squirms,
Do the Wednesday morning wiggle
With the Wednesday morning worms.

They gather in the crevices
Between the sidewalk cracks
And they dance in wormy puddles
With the sunrise on their backs.

I taught them all the can-can
(They had trouble with the kicks)
But they dance a tangled tango
And they twist a knotty twist.

So come and greet the sunrise
When the puddles start to churn,
Come and dance the wormy wiggle
With the Wednesday morning worms.

Escape

I went to the market
To buy me a pig
I put him in the pot
But he danced a jig.
He danced in the skillet
He danced in the pan
He danced with the kettle
And away he ran.

I went to the market
To buy me a goose
I put her in the pot
But she wiggled loose.
She wiggled in the noodles
She wiggled in the stew
She wiggled in the pudding
And away she flew.

I went to the market
To buy me a trout
I put him in the pot
But he jumped back out.
He jumped in the jelly
He jumped in the jam
He jumped in the water
And away he swam.

I went to the market
To buy me a hen
I put her in the pot
But she scratched again.
She scratched on the counter
She scratched on the floor
She scratched at the window
And away she tore.

I went to the market
To buy a fat duck
I put him in the pot
But he got stuck.
He stuck to the table
He stuck to the cup
He stuck around for dinner
So I ate him up!

The Cat Who Went Moo

There once was a cat who went Moo.
She said, "Oh, what can I do?
I should go Meow
Not Moo like a cow,"
So sadly she cried, "Moo hoo."

How Preposterous

Margaret's so preposterous
She swallowed a rhinoceros!
She ate him up from tail to snout
(Except the parts she spit back out.)
She munched his toes and crunched his feet,
She spread grape jelly on the meat.
She stuffed his horn with pickled eel
And fried the wrinkles on his heel.
She dipped the bones in sour cream
And licked his knobby knuckles clean.
At last she ate his tangled hair
And then the rhino wasn't there.
How awful, how preposterous!
She ate the *whole* rhinoceros
And didn't share with me.

Bounce

I have a friend and his name is Bounce,
And he weighs a ton if he weighs an ounce.
But Bounce can bounce both up and down,
Why Bounce can bounce the best in town!

And Bounce wears boots as big as boats
And a black beret and a big black coat.
And Bounce can bounce like a rubber ball,
His bouncing's really off the wall.

He can bounce a ball, he can bounce a man,
He can bounce a flea off an old tin can.
He can bounce so high that he won't come down,
He can bounce from here to Charlottetown!

Renee

Renee, Renee,
Has nothing to say
Her tongue is tied up in a knot.
A tongue twister tangled
Her tongue in quadrangles
And what she could say she cannot, cannot,
And what she could say she cannot.

Renee, Renee,
Has something to say
For she knew just what to do.
Put her foot in her mouth
And the knot, it came out,
Now the knot's in the lace of her shoe, her shoe,
The knot's in the lace of her shoe.

Garbage Can Dan

Garbage Can Dan
Is a marvellous man,
'Cause he finds terrific treasures
In the old trash can.

He found a piece of screening
And he made a fishing net,
He found a can of soup once
And he made the alphabet.

He found a pair of chicken wings
And tied them to his back,
He flew to Nova Scotia
With his treasures in a sack!

Margo's Car

Margo's car goes
Sailing through the sky
Where the morning star goes
After it goes by.
Where the morning star goes
Margo and I go
For only Margo's car knows
Where goes the sky.

Margo's car goes
Wading on the shore
Where the sandy bar goes
When the sea's no more.
Where the sandy bar goes
Margo and I go
For only Margo's car knows
Where goes the shore.

Margo's car goes
Sliding through a song
Where the blue guitar goes
When the music's gone.
Where the blue guitar goes
Margo and I go
For only Margo's car knows
Where goes the song.

Margo's car goes
Singing back to me
Though it isn't far, there's
Everything to see.
Though it isn't far, there
Margo and I go
For nobody else knows
Where go we.

Peter the Plumber

With a crash bang, rattle bang, clinkity clink,
Peter the Plumber is fixing the sink.
　　He plunges with his plunger
　　And the gurgling noises start,
　　He crawls beneath the counter
　　And he takes the pipes apart.
　　He let me hold the hammer
　　'Til I hit him on the toe,
　　He let me turn the water on
　　But then he had to go.
But all I have to do to make him visit me again
Is chew sticky bubble gum and stick it down the drain.

Hiccups

Pass me the potatoes
And dish me up some stew,
Bring on out the broccoli
With butter on it too.
But if it's peas you're passing
Pass right by me please!
'Cause I always get the hiccups
Whenever I eat peas.

You can tuck them in a casserole
Or mash them on my toast,
You can hide them in a meat pie
Or underneath the roast.
You can toss them in a salad
Or cover them with cheese,
But I cannot hide the hiccups
Whenever I eat peas.

I've tried to eat them cooked
And I've tried to eat them raw
And I've even tried to chew them
Without opening my jaw.
But I can feel it tickle
As if I'm going to sneeze,
Look out! Here come the hiccups
Whenever I eat peas! (hic)

Gravity

It doesn't matter if I pour
Water from the second floor
Onto my sister Eleanor,
    'Cause it's not me, it's gravity,
    Gravity, that's all,
    'Cause even though I dropped it
    Gravity made it fall.

It doesn't matter if I drop
Porridge from the table top
And let my puppy be the mop,
    'Cause it's not me, it's gravity,
    Gravity, that's all,
    'Cause even though I dropped it
    Gravity made it fall.

But now my father thinks it keen
To drop me on the trampoline
And as I bounce back up I scream,
    "Oh, it's not me, it's gravity,
    Gravity, that's all."
    'Cause even though he dropped me
    Gravity made me fall.

Street Names

I rode my bike to Queen Street
But I couldn't find the Queen,
Though I found an empty bottle
And a broken-down machine,
And a penny with her picture
But her face was turning green.
So why is it called Queen Street
If it hasn't got a Queen?

I took a bus to King Street
But I didn't see the King,
Though I saw somebody singing
With a washtub and a string
And I looked inside a sewer
But I couldn't see a thing.
So why is it called King Street
If it hasn't got a King?

I rode down to Saint George Street
But Saint George was not around,
Though I know he fights with dragons
And I heard a dragon sound.
I'll chase dragons on my bicycle,
I'll run them to the ground.
I'll slay dragons on Saint George Street
When Saint George cannot be found.

Revolving

The building on the corner
Has a revolving door.
I spun it round one morning
And I found out what it's for:
It's not for going in
And it's not for going out,
It's just for going round and round
And round and round about.

I can turn it all alone,
I can turn it with a friend,
I can turn it round forever
And I'll never reach the end.
'Cause it's always going in
And it's always going out,
It's always going round and round
And round and round about.

I think I'm getting dizzy,
I think I'm getting dazed,
I think I'll keep on spinning
For another sixty days.
'Cause I'm never going in
And I'm never going out,
I'm only going round and round
And round and round about.

Looking for Holes

I lost my bottom button hole
I don't know where it's gone,
It must have fallen off me
When I put my sweater on.

I was doing up my buttons
Beginning at the chin,
But the one down at the bottom
Had no hole to put it in.

I checked inside my pockets
And found a hole or two,
But not the one I'm missing
So it must have fallen through.

I found a hole for marbles
That roll across the floor,
And I found a hole for spying
In my sister's bedroom door.

I found a lot of other holes
But not the one I dropped,
I even found one like it
On my sweater, at the top!